This book is given with love:

_____

_____

READ & PLAY:
3 cats are hiding on each page.
See if you can find them as you read.
(Ears, tails, and clouds count!)

DOG FOOD is for CATS

ILLUSTRATED BY
Javier Gimenez Ratti

WRITTEN BY
Jason Kutasi

Piper woke up hungry
at his old Kentucky farm...
The warmth of the sun
as his morning alarm.

His little tummy grumbled
with a rumble so deep...
It woke all the rabbits
who were still trying to sleep.

Staring down at his food
in a bright yellow dish...
No more kibble for breakfast
was Piper's everyday wish.

Dreaming of cookies,
chocolate cake, and other treats...
Piper licked his drooling lips
at the thought of all those sweets.

"I am done eating kibble.
I'd rather eat grass!
Or pizza with mustard...
Dog Food is for Cats!"

A soft buzzing bumbled,
    as a swarm of bees drew near.
"Good morning young Piper,"
    they buzzed in his ear.

"I am tired of kibble,"
  Piper told his bee friends.
"Follow us to the fields
  where the food never ends."

A quick sniff of the flowers,
Piper sneezed an "Ahh-Choo!"
The bees quickly noticed,
"Nectar isn't for you."

A black and white cow
must know how to feast.
You don't get that fat
unless you eat like a beast.

Piper made a sour face
with a mouthful of grass...
"This isn't my thing.
I'm gonna have to pass."

With a "Neigh" in the distance,
Piper thought, "Of course!"
The best barnyard meal
must be eaten by a horse.

Piper expected a big breakfast,
maybe eggs and some bacon.
But he only saw hay here,
he'd been sorely mistaken.

Walking through the woods
  Piper spotted a small bunny.
It hopped by in a flash
  laughing at something funny.

Triggered by instinct,
    Piper quickly gave chase.
He was one tired puppy,
    having lost the bunny race.

Awakened by an owl
with a "Hooooo" from above...
She offered her mousy meal,
a gesture made with love.

A fox crept from the bushes
eyeing his next catch.
Piper sure does like chicken,
but they peck and they scratch!

Piper found some pigs,
  rolling in the mud with a squeal.
Kibble is pretty bad,
  but slop is the WORST meal!

At the edge of the farm,
   fresh corn grows aplenty.
But this donkey wouldn't share;
   he wouldn't give Piper any.

Goats are super friendly
and will share a bag of feed.
"But kibble made for goats
isn't exactly what I need."

So back to the kibble
the farmer delivered at dawn...
In the shiny yellow bowl
that was still on the lawn.

Hungrier than ever,
   Piper scarfed down his food...
Filling his tummy with kibble,
   the best meal he'd ever chewed.

Piper licked the bowl clean,
content as can be...

One tired puppy...
fell asleep under the tree.